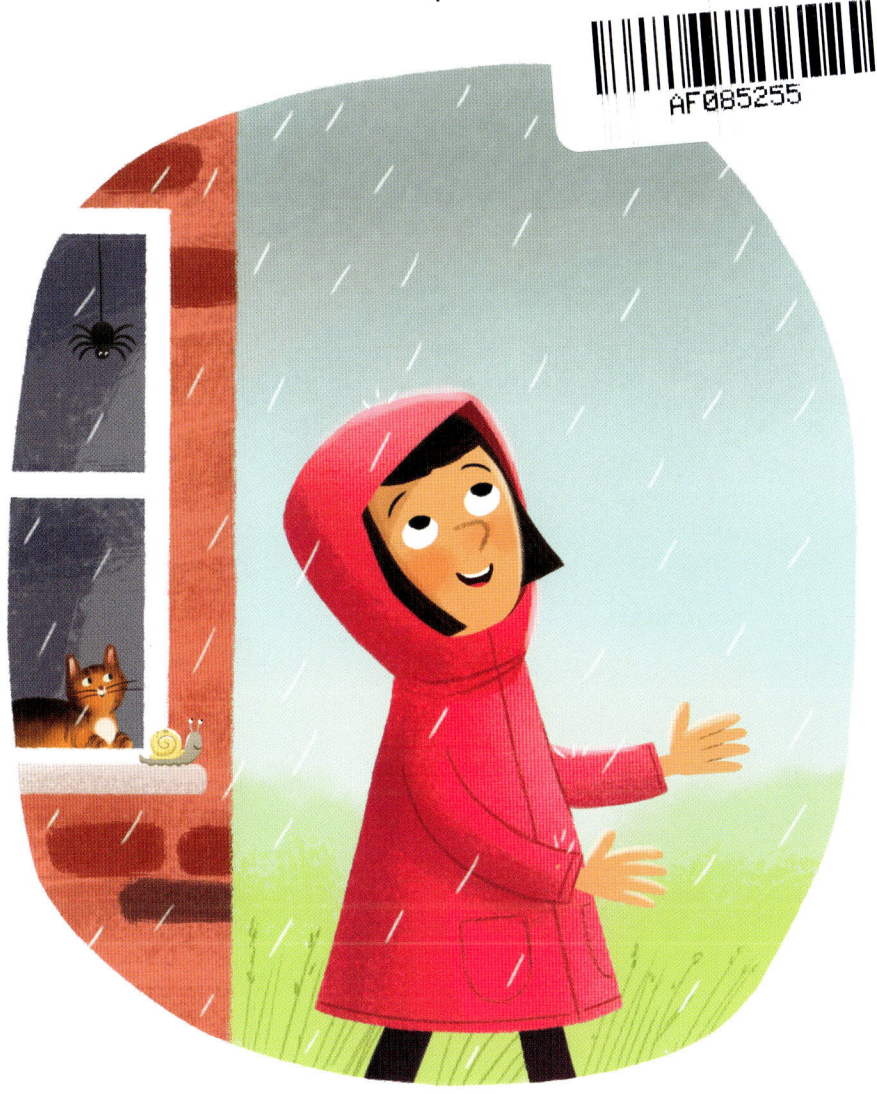

Rain...

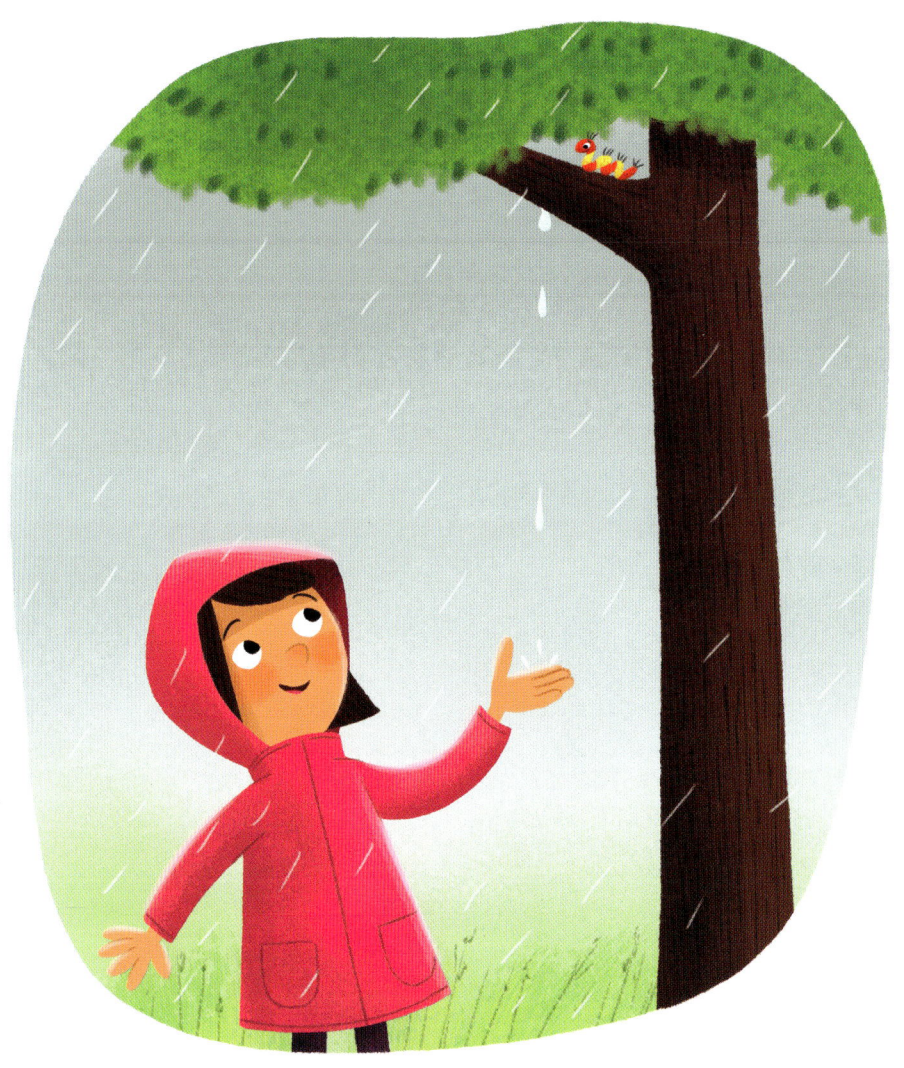

drips and drops.

It splishes and splashes!

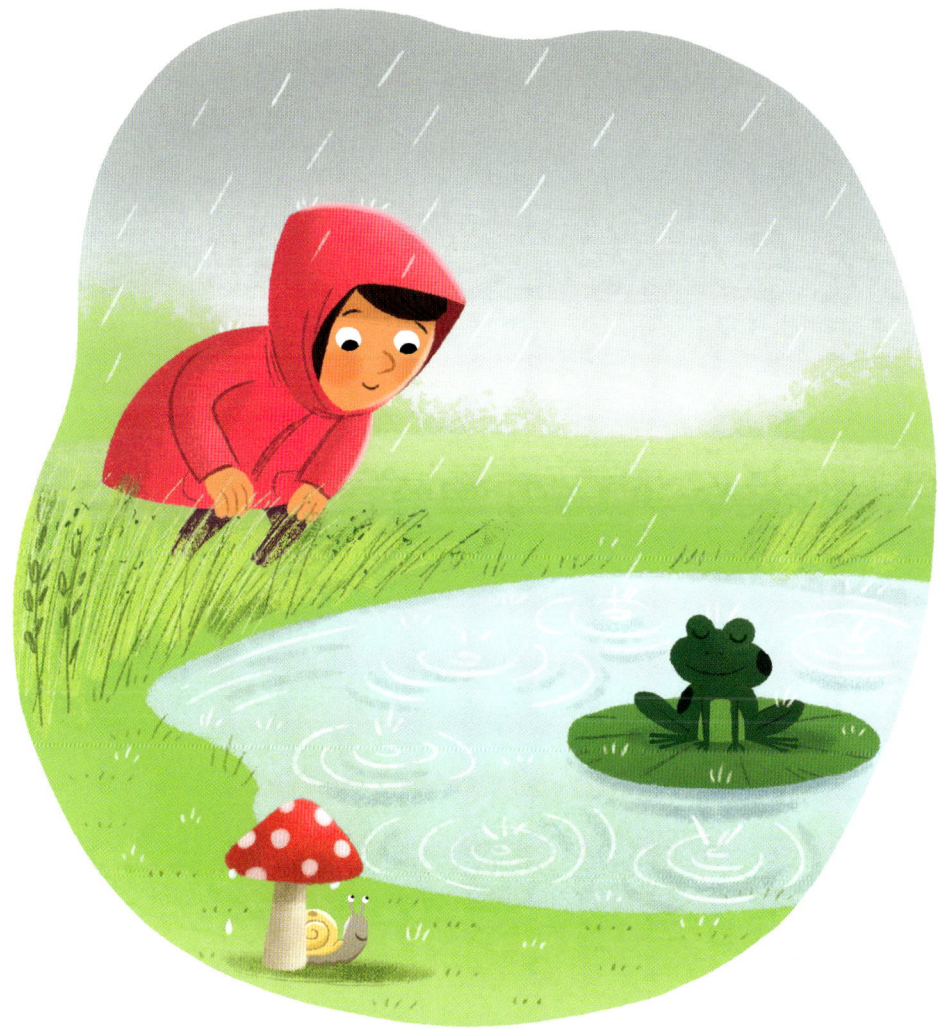

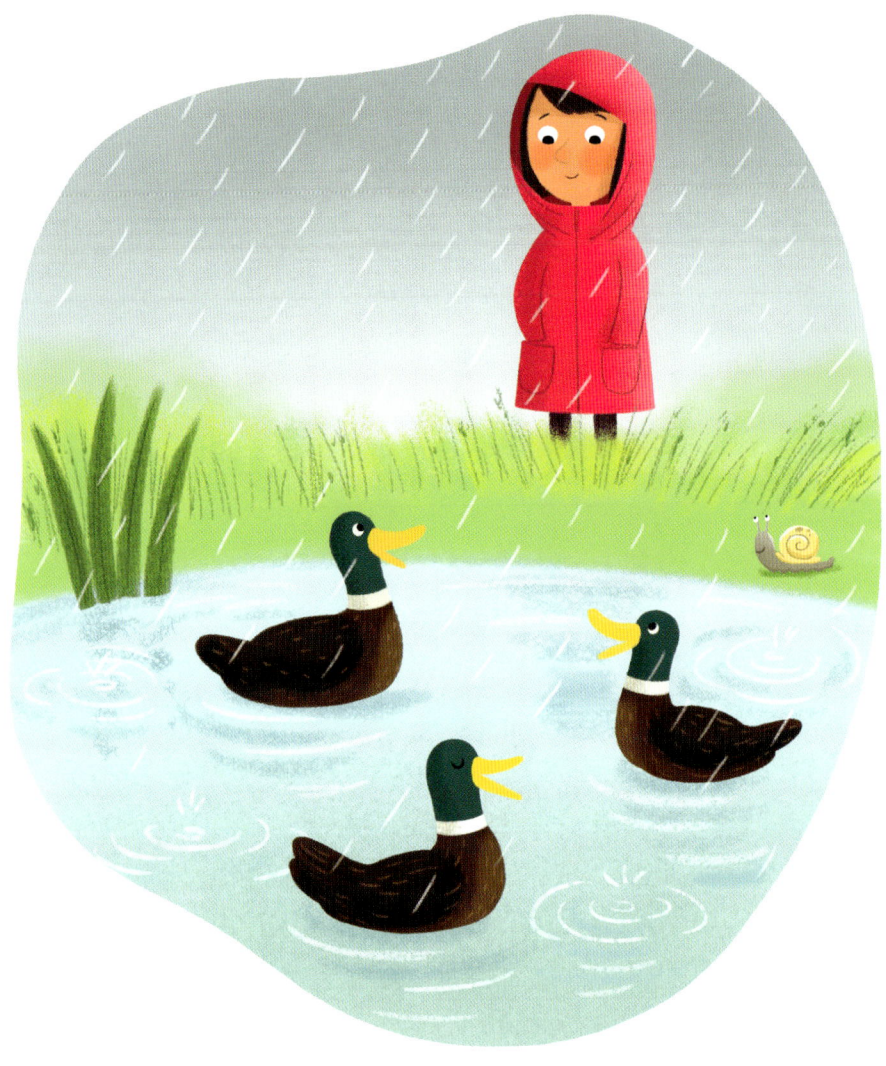

The ducks quack

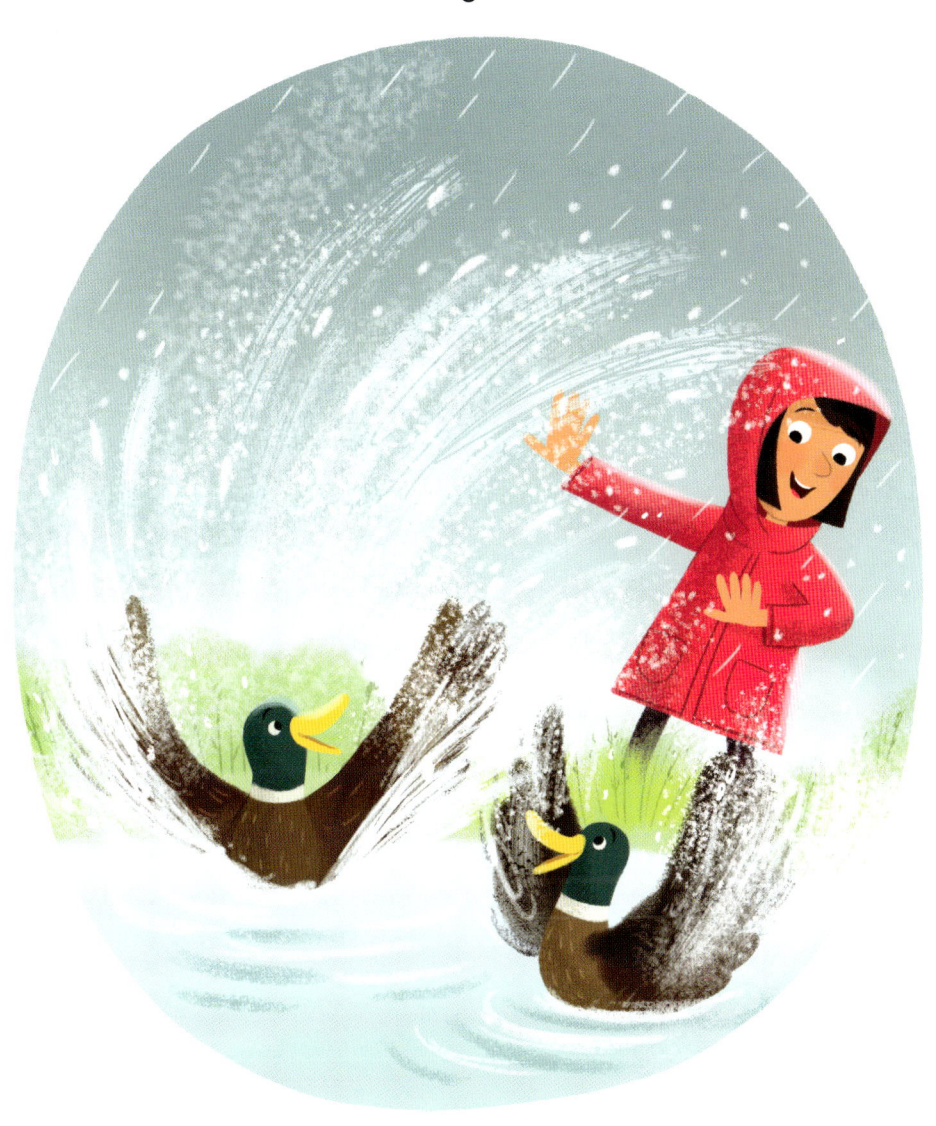

and flap!

Big red boots

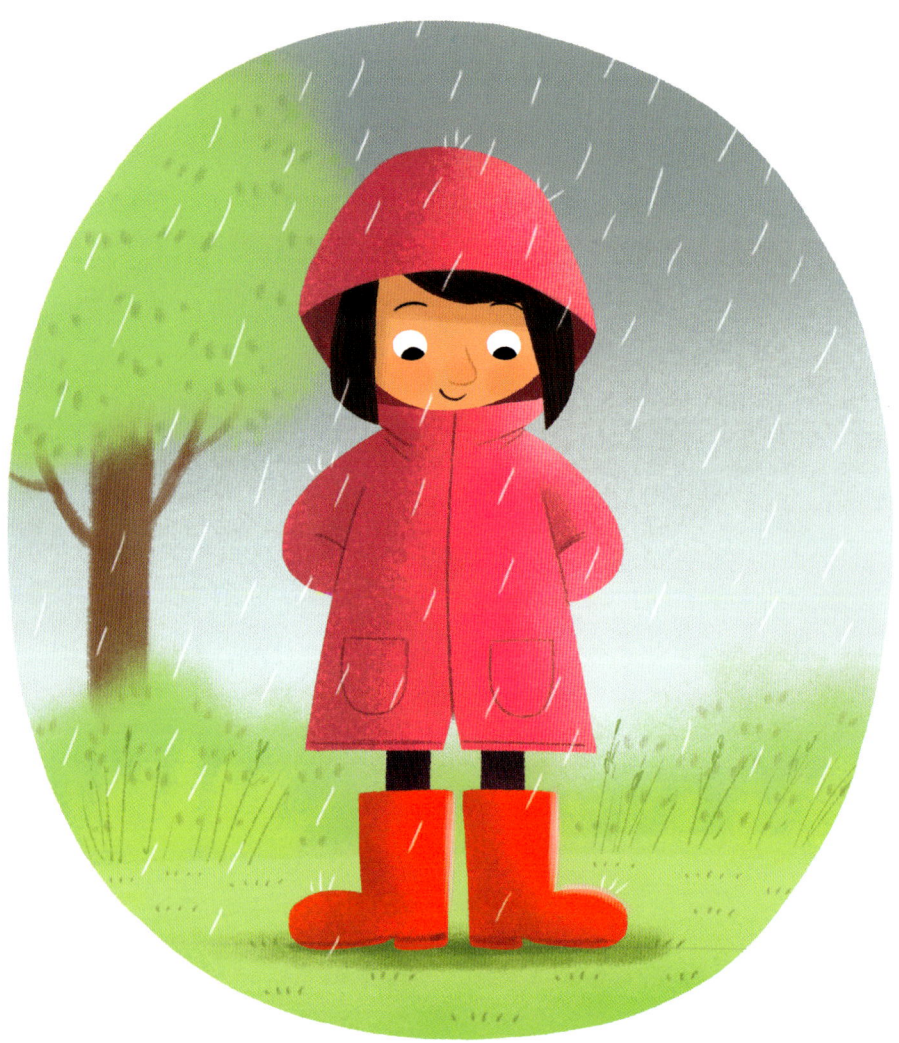

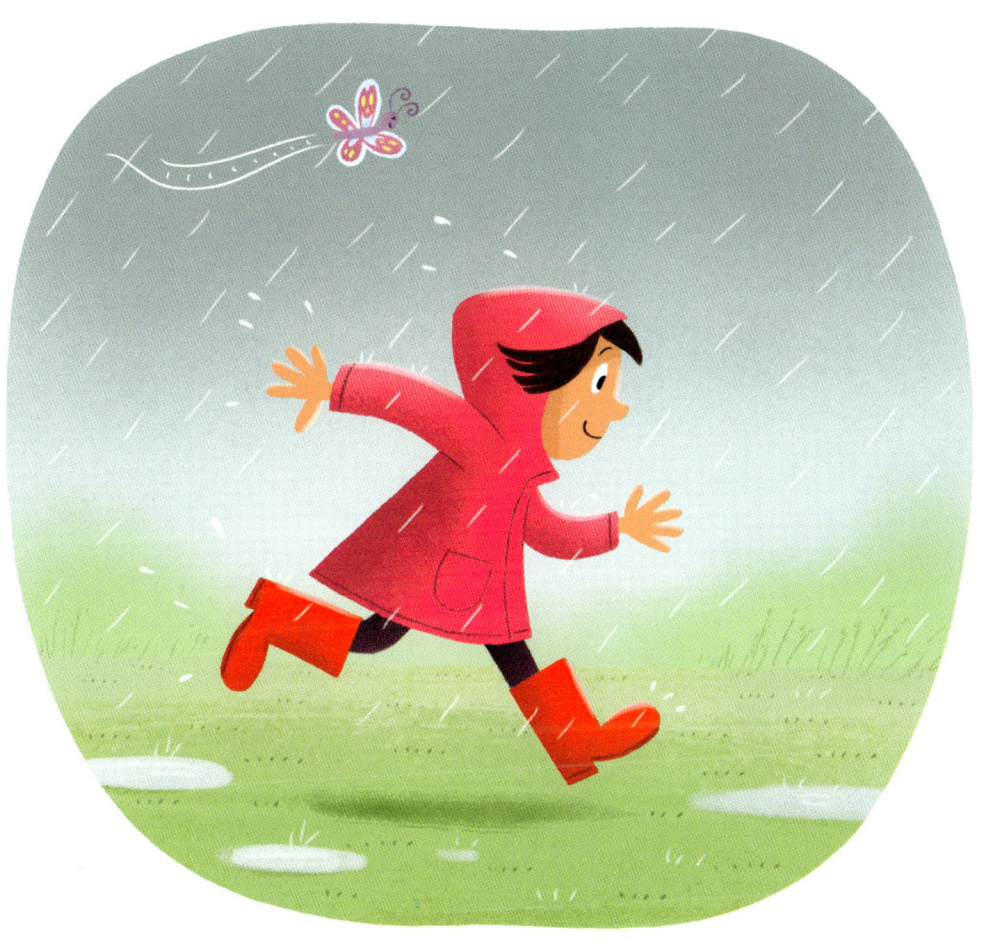

are perfect for...

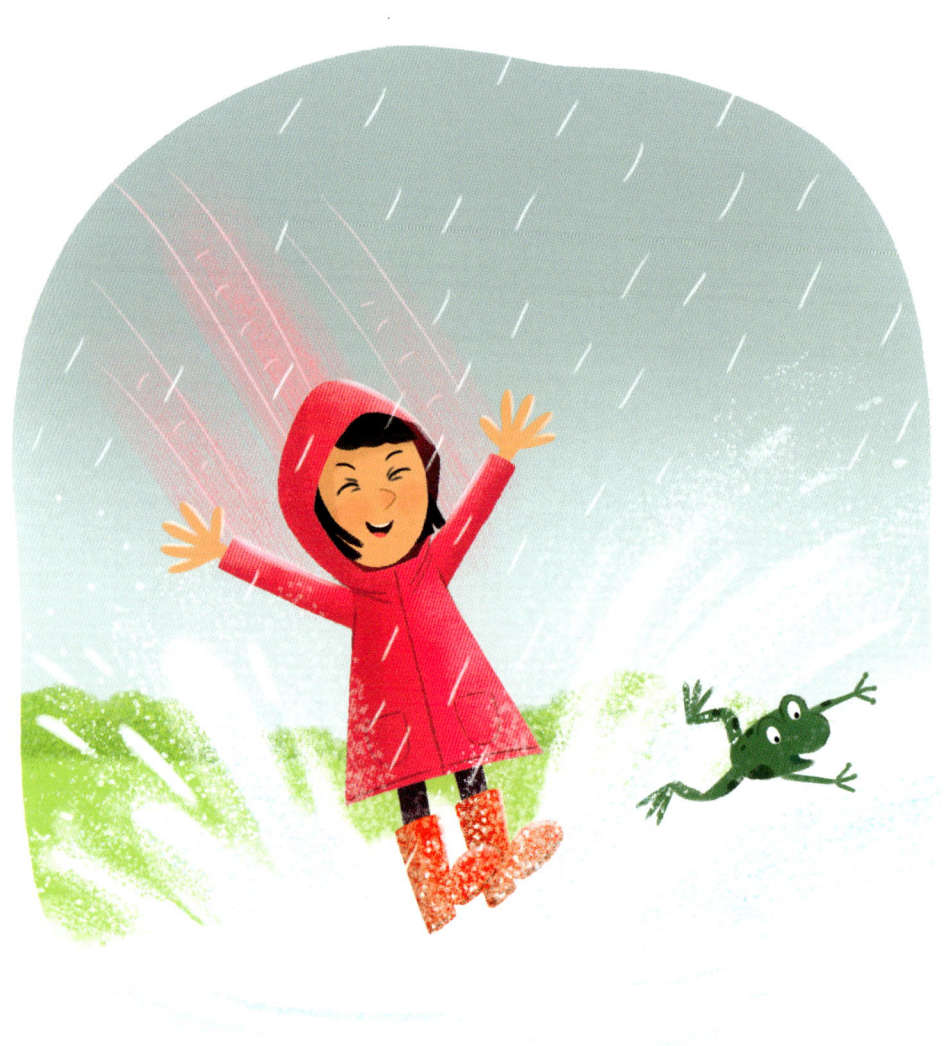

splashing!

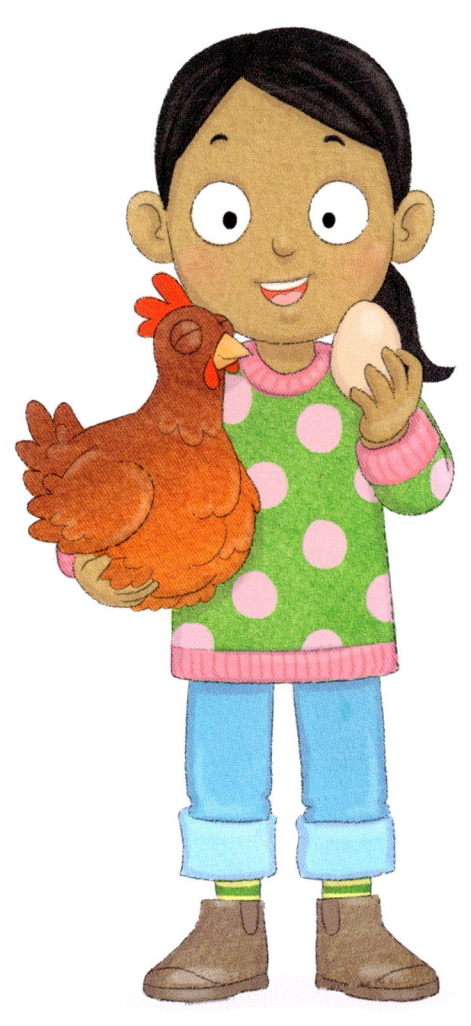

an egg!

Hinda's hen, and...

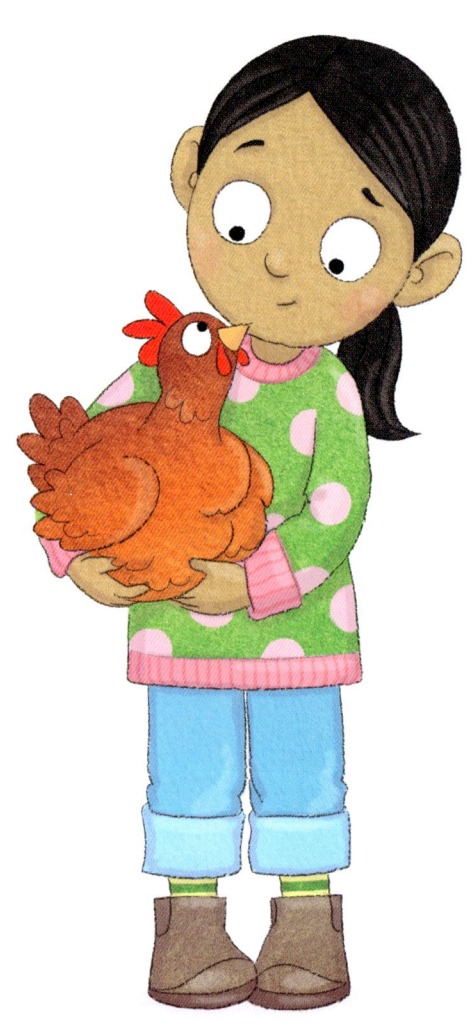

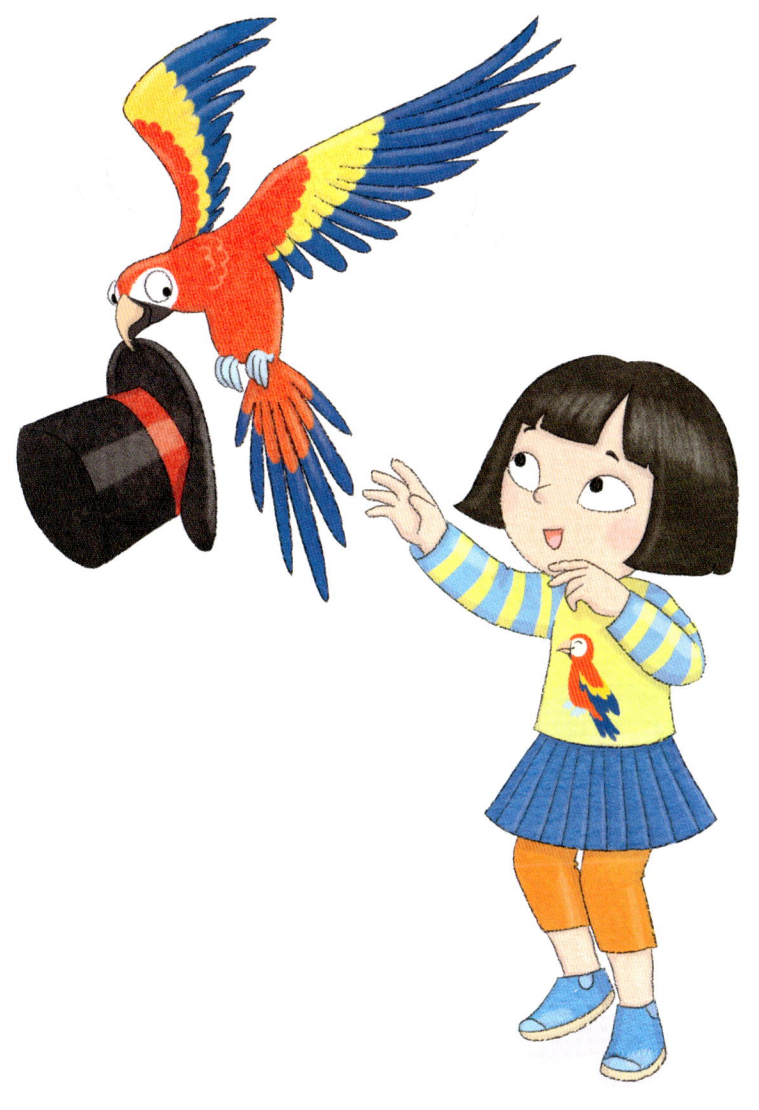

Cheng's parrot

Adam's rabbit

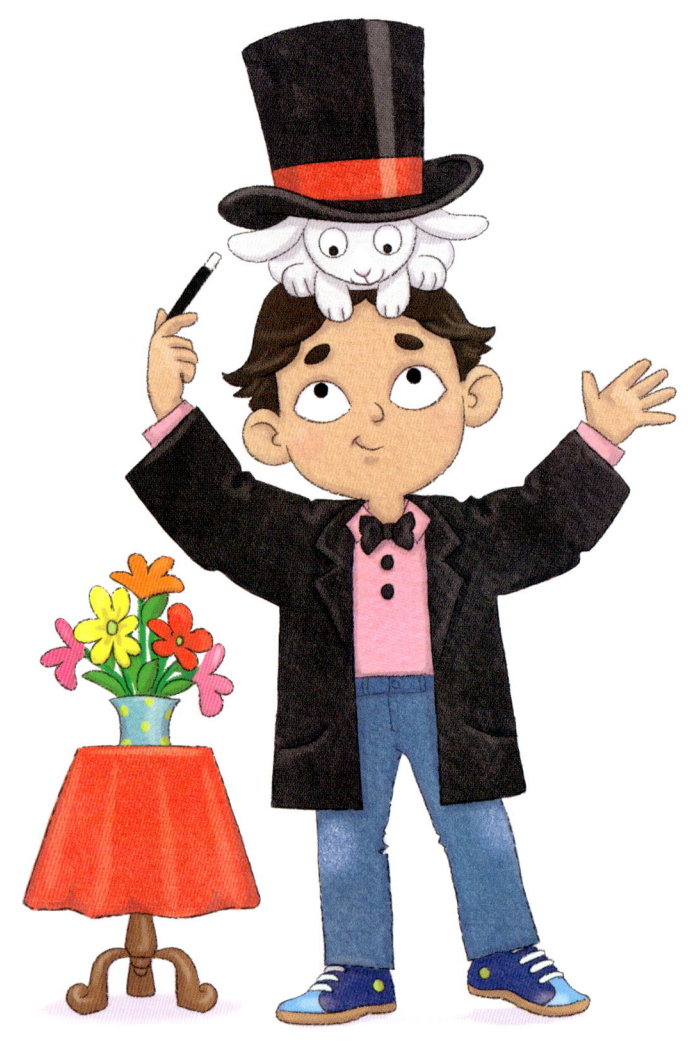

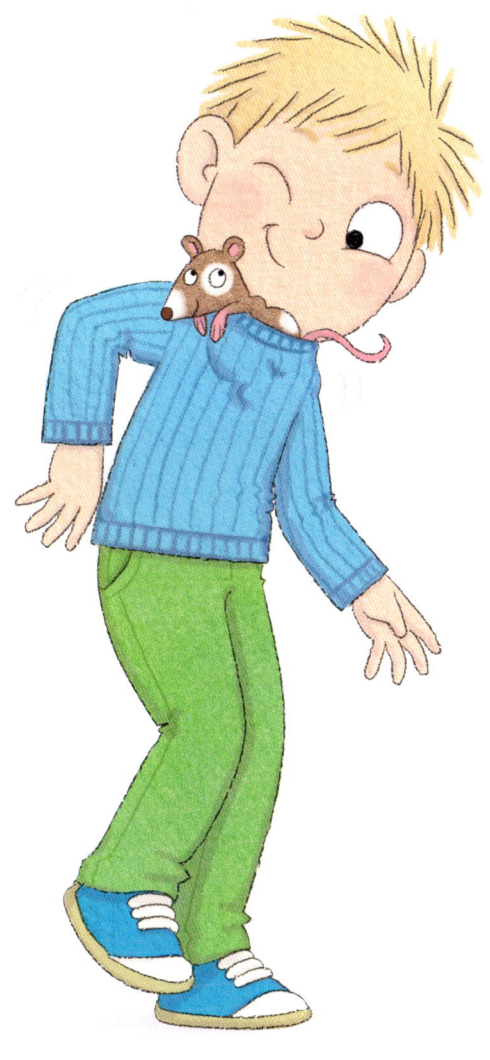

Will's rat

Zack's dog

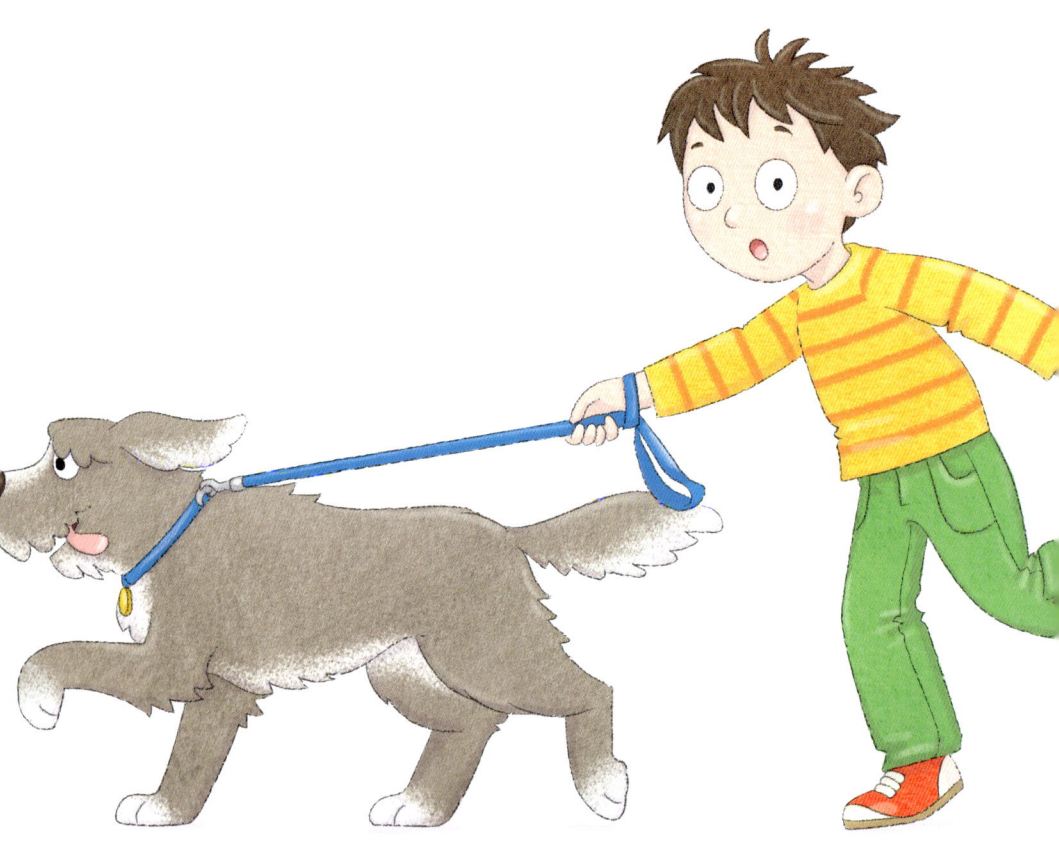

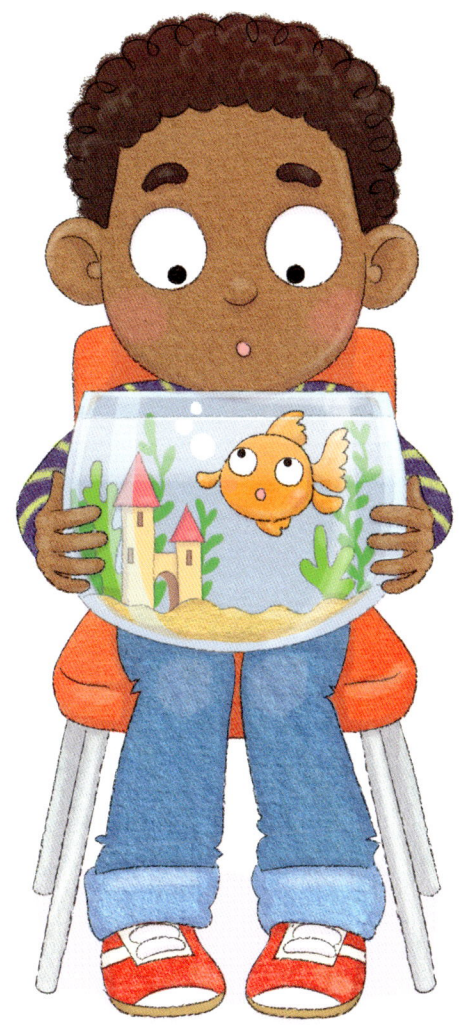

Seth's fish

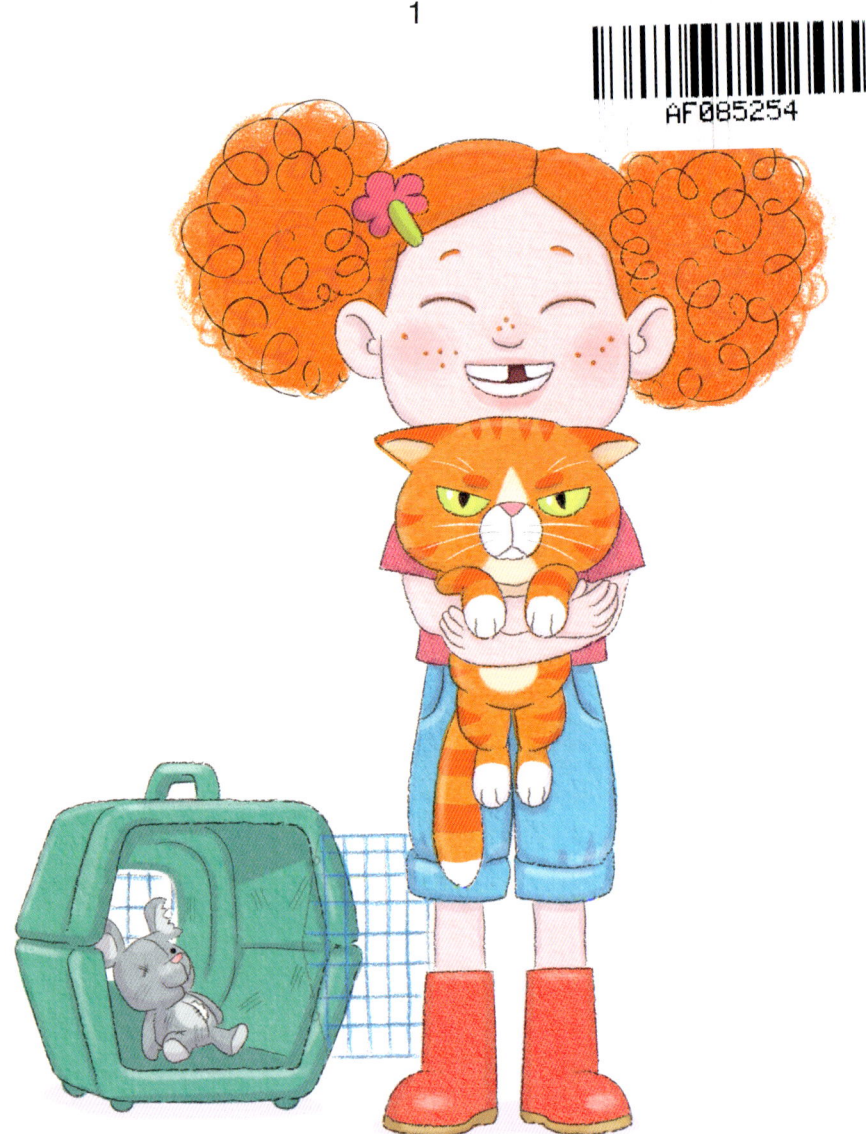

Jen's cat